RavirA
RULER OF THE
UNDERWORLD

With special thanks to Michael Ford

*For Nick Williams, the biggest
Beast Quest fan*

www.beastquest.co.uk

ORCHARD BOOKS
338 Euston Road, London NW1 3BH
Orchard Books Australia
Level 17/207 Kent St, Sydney, NSW 2000

A Paperback Original
First published in Great Britain in 2011

Beast Quest is a registered trademark of Beast Quest Limited
Series created by Working Partners Limited, London

A CIP catalogue record for this book is available
from the British Library.

ISBN 978 1 40831 322 0

9 10 8

Printed and bound by CPI Group (UK) Ltd, Croydon, CR0 4YY

The paper and board used in this paperback are natural recyclable
products made from wood grown in sustainable forests.
The manufacturing processes conform to the environmental
regulations of the country of origin.

Orchard Books is a division of Hachette Children's Books,
an Hachette UK company.

www.hachette.co.uk

RavirA
RULER OF THE
UNDERWORLD

BY ADAM BLADE

ORCHARD

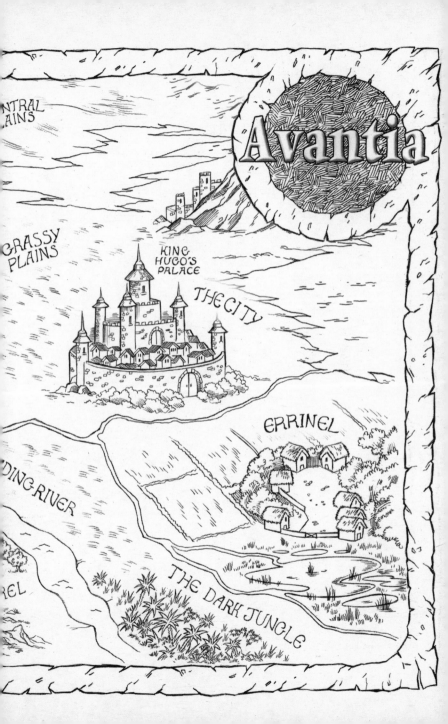

STORY ONE

The moon! By its light, our mistress has awoken. I lick my fangs and fur. The hair on my spine stands erect. Every sense is alive. My nostrils flare as I smell the air. The time has come. Ravira will be Queen again.

Fear spreads like an infection through the kingdom; I feel it. The foolish humans have sent one hero already, and we have tasted his blood. If he was their greatest warrior, then Avantia will soon fall. The whole kingdom will come under our thrall, and I will enjoy the taste of human blood again.

I send out a howl: Come, fellow Hounds, let us hunt. Let us take all this land for our queen.

Humans, fear us. Heroes, tremble. The Hounds of Avantia have been unleashed!

CHAPTER ONE

A FATE WORSE THAN DEATH

The morning had started peacefully, with sunlight glinting through the windows of Tom's chamber at King Hugo's palace. He was polishing the magical tokens on his shield when a pounding fist shook the door. He ran to pull it open. Aduro stood there, his face ashen and drawn.

"Terrible news!" panted Aduro.

Fear prickled at Tom. "Is it Elenna?"

Aduro shook his head and entered
the room, then sank down onto a
stool. His shoulders hunched. Tom
had never seen him so disturbed.

"Taladon's in danger," said Aduro.
"It may already be too late."

"But I saw my father last night at
the King's Banquet," Tom said.

Aduro looked at him. "Late last

night, we received word of a disturbance in the village of Shrayton," he said, "between the Forest of Fear and the Western Ocean. I asked Taladon to investigate, and used my magic to transport him there…"

Tom knew Shrayton, a quiet place where farmers and their families lived. "What kind of disturbance?" asked Tom.

"A terrible evil," muttered Aduro. "A cursed Beast – Ravira." He spoke the name in a whisper, and Tom felt as though a cold breeze had crept into the chamber. Could there really be another Beast lurking in Avantia?

"I've never heard of Ravira," he said.

Aduro wrung his hands together. "Many have not," he said. "Even former Masters of the Beasts never heard the name – and with good reason. Ravira is the foulest, cruellest Beast to ever stalk this kingdom. But she is supposed to be contained within the Avantian underworld…"

Tom had never seen Aduro look so agitated – nor so worried. "What happened to my father?" he asked, dreading the answer.

Aduro sighed. "I know that Taladon was bitten by a Hound of Avantia – one of the men cursed to be a dog-servant to Ravria until the end of time."

Aduro's eyes widened and he slapped his forehead, looking past Tom and talking to himself. "Of course! Ravira must have found out a way to get her dog servants out of the underworld. My word – this is bad… This is very bad…"

Tom fought to control his emotions. "Is my father dead?"

Aduro stood up and placed a hand on his shoulder.

"Not dead, Tom. Worse."

A noise at the door made them both turn. Elenna stood there grinning.

"Tom, you should have seen Silver chasing the ducks..." She trailed off and her smile vanished as she saw their grim faces. "What's going on?"

"You should hear this, too," said Aduro. "Taladon has been bitten by one of Ravira's Hounds." The wizard extended a finger and pointed towards the wall of the chamber where a tapestry hung. At once, the woven cloth shimmered, and in its place Tom saw a vision of his father. Taladon stood over a bed, where a

man lay curled into a ball and
shivering. As Taladon reached out
to touch the man's shoulder, he
snapped his head around as if
surprised. A pale blur leapt at
Taladon, throwing him to the floor.
Tom saw his father wrestle with
a dog that looked twice the size of
Silver. He caught the flash of
glistening teeth and red eyes

before the vision faded.

"Is he all right?" Tom asked desperately.

"He lives," said Aduro. "But in the light of tonight's moon, Taladon will change. Unless you defeat Ravira."

"Change?" Tom and Elenna spoke together.

Aduro gripped Tom's shoulder more tightly, and looked into his eyes. "Your father will become a Hound of Avantia – he will be cursed to live out the rest of eternity as a vicious dog, serving the Beast."

From the stables across the palace courtyard, a dog howled. The sound carried through the window and seemed to hang in the air, eerie and menacing. Tom rushed to the table and snatched up his sword-belt. "We have to go at once!" he said. "I won't let my father meet that fate."

"I'll fetch my bow," said Elenna, darting out the door.

Tom grabbed his shield and ran to the stables to saddle Storm. His faithful stallion snorted with nerves, as if sensing Tom's anxiety. Elenna arrived breathlessly as he was leading the horse out. Silver stood obediently at her side, his tongue lolling.

Aduro was waiting for them at the gates. "I can use my magic to get you closer," said the wizard, "but as Ravira's power grows, my spells are less effective. You'll be on your own in Shrayton."

Tom placed a foot in the stirrup and swung his leg over the saddle. Elenna climbed up behind him. "Thank you," Tom said to Aduro.

"Good luck," said the wizard. "But

remember, Tom, this isn't only about your father. Now that Ravira is strong enough to send her Hounds to the surface, there is no telling where they will roam. They could travel anywhere. The entire kingdom is at risk."

He waved his hand and the courtyard disappeared.

Tom and Elenna found themselves on the outskirts of the Forest of Fear. Tom looked to the stars to get his bearings. "We're still half a day's ride from Shrayton!" he said. "Ravira's magic must be more powerful than Aduro realised. Faster, Storm!"

The stallion whinnied and charged off at a gallop through the fields, his hooves thundering.

"You're pushing him too hard!" said Elenna, gripping Tom's waist.

He held the reins tightly, pulling back to jump Storm over a small brook. He twisted in the saddle to see Silver leap as well, a few paces behind.

"I have no choice," he yelled. "If we don't get there before nightfall…"

Storm's powerful legs carried them onwards. As they rode, an awful vision from the chamber leapt up in Tom's mind: the terrifying glimpse he'd had of Ravira's Hound. How many were there? Perhaps the whole village had been bitten!

The air blasted through his tunic, as Tom watched the glowing orange orb of the Avantian sun sink ever lower.

Finally they burst onto a muddy track marked with other hoofprints.

"This must be the way," said Elenna.

Tom spied trails of smoke from distant chimneys to the north, and took one hand from the rein to slap Storm's muscular neck.

"You're doing well, boy!" he told his stallion. "We're nearly there!"

Still he didn't let up the gallop. Tom remembered how Aduro had spoken the Beast's name with real fear. *If Ravira rules over all the Hounds*, he thought, *she must be a powerful adversary. Perhaps the deadliest yet.*

A shape appeared on the horizon, and Tom let Storm sink back to a canter, so that he could draw his sword. But the figure was just a boy, standing beside a gatepost on the edge of a village and shielding his eyes from the setting sun. Tom sheathed his blade again and slowed to a trot. Storm's flanks heaved with exhaustion, and even Silver's head was lowered as he caught his breath.

"Are you Tom?" asked the boy. "Thank goodness!" He looked back over his shoulder.

Tom frowned. "How do you know my name?"

The boy seemed taken aback, and even a little afraid. "Taladon told me to expect a boy and girl on a black horse." He looked nervously at Silver. "And a grey wolf. I'm Jacob."

Tom leapt down from the saddle. "Where's my father ?" he asked.

Jacob pointed towards a group of low buildings. "We helped the wounded warrior to the old stable-block," he said. "It's a little way from the rest of village. Follow me."

They dismounted and followed the boy to the stables. A couple of hundred paces away, the village houses squatted like shadows in the dusk light. Apart from the trails of smoke, Shrayton seemed eerily quiet. The last of the sun's rays seeped away, and Tom made out the dim orb of the moon across to the east.

At the stable door, Fleetfoot, his father's stallion, stood patiently waiting. Tom had never seen this noble horse without his father by its side. He pushed down the rising panic in his chest and stroked the stallion's long nose. "There, there, boy. We're here now."

Elenna squeezed Tom's arm. "Come on. Let's find your father."

"Quick! Inside!" Jacob hissed, hurrying them around the side of the stable. He pointed towards the village, where a crowd of people carrying torches had emerged.

"We mean them no harm," whispered Elenna.

"They patrol the streets looking for people who've been bitten," said Jacob. "They don't know he's here."

The boy's hand trembled as he

pushed against the stable door. It swung open with a creak. Silver whined and Elenna ruffled his neck. "Wait here," she told her wolf.

The air was thick with the smell of straw. The roof had partially collapsed and moonlight hung in pale shafts. Towards the back of the stable stood the remains of a brick chimney, and a dark figure lay curled against it. Tom recognised Taladon's hunched form, breathing quickly in shallow pants. "Father?"

As he moved closer, the moonlight caught the glint of chains, snaking from shackles at Taladon's wrists to metal hoops embedded in the bricks. Anger flared in Tom's heart. He shot a glance at Jacob. "What have you done to him?" he asked. "Why have you locked him up?"

"I wouldn't go closer if I were you," said Jacob, cringing against the wall.

Tom caught a movement in the corner of his eye.

"Look out!" Elenna cried.

Tom spun around and saw his father spring from the ground towards him, suddenly illuminated in the moonlight. The chains rattled and pulled tight as Taladon's hands clawed the air. Tom fell back and gasped with horror. Taladon's face was twisted with rage, his eyes bloodshot and full of hate. His teeth seemed sharper, trailing drool over his filthy tunic. The strong fingers that grasped and flexed towards Tom ended in long yellow nails.

Then Taladon uttered a strange growl and collapsed to his knees. His energy seemed to have evaporated,

leaving him a crumpled figure on the
stable floor. Thick hair coated the
back of his neck. *That wasn't there
before*, Tom thought. When Taladon
looked up at him again, his eyes were
red-rimmed and watery. He panted
with exhaustion and hastily pulled at
the cuffs of his tunic to hide the curls
of hair that sprouted there.

"What's happened to you?" Tom
asked, hearing the quiver in his voice.

"You shouldn't have come," Taladon
croaked. "It's too late."

CHAPTER TWO

VILLAGE OF THE DAMNED

Tom struggled to his feet with
Elenna's help. His legs felt weak, and
his stomach twisted. He glimpsed the
wound on Taladon's upper thigh,
where his trousers were torn open
with tooth-marks and caked brown
with dried blood. His father retreated
back to the bricks in jerking
movements, dragging his chains
with him.

"Father..." Tom said, his voice cracking. He took a few steps forward, but then stopped when his father's shaggy head snapped up again. A light burned in his eyes that looked like the fire Tom had seen in the eyes of wild animals.

"Stay away!" hissed Taladon.

"But—"

"Don't come closer! I can't be trusted. I can feel the infection spreading, getting stronger all the time." Taladon reached out trembling clawed fingers to Tom, then snatched his hand back.

Tom advanced a step towards Jacob. "You should have kept him out of the moonlight," he muttered, glancing up at the holes in the roof.

"He wasn't to know," Elenna said.

"I did what he asked," said Jacob

uncertainly, still hovering by the door. "He insisted I lock him up with shackles from the jailhouse. He'd seen what happened to the others when they were bitten."

"Others?" said Elenna.

Jacob nodded. "The other villagers. They all turn, the night after they're bitten. Then they disappear. Taladon knew he wouldn't be able to control it."

"How many have been infected?" asked Tom.

"I don't know," said Jacob. "Six, ten, maybe more. Everyone else has locked themselves indoors for the night, or they go out in groups with weapons. The Hounds seem to disappear in the daytime."

Tom looked at his father. *He's not completely changed yet. But he does not have long… Once the moon rises…* Tom shook his head, not finishing his own thought. He couldn't bear to think of his father completing this hideous transformation. Taladon's lips twitched over bright white fangs. *I will not let him become one of them.*

Tom thought about using the talon in his shield. He'd been given six tokens from the first six Beast's he'd liberated. Epos's talon allowed him to cure small injuries. *But it won't work against this level of enchantment*, he thought bitterly.

"There's only one way," he muttered. "We have to fight Ravira."

"No!" Taladon roared. He became suddenly wild again, prowling towards Tom on all fours, his hair hanging over his face. "Flee to the city, my son. Run while you can!"

Tom straightened his shoulders.
"I'm not running anywhere!" he said.

Taladon groaned and snarled in pain. With a sound like crunching twigs, his back arched, splitting his tunic open. Elenna gasped as, instead of skin, the ridges of a hairy hide burst through.

Taladon stared at Tom, his eyes almost completely red. "Be careful, Tom! Don't be tricked as I was. Ravira is a cunning enemy." His father's words came out in a low, sinister hiss and Tom noticed the flecks of spit at the corners of Taladon's mouth. His enchantment grew worse with every passing moment.

Tom crouched down, so his eyes were level with his father's. He knew this was dangerous, but he had to see into Taladon's eyes – he had to make sure he understood the next question. "Where is Ravira's lair?"

Taladon jerked his head, and opened his mouth to speak. "It's deep…"

The words turned into a growl, as Taladon's jaw jutted forward, stretching into the shape of a muzzle. His nostrils flattened to become a snout. He tipped back his head and gave an awful howl.

"Come on, Tom!" said Elenna. "We have to go. He can't help us now."

Tom backed away from the creature, never pulling his gaze from the thing that had been his father only a few moments ago. *I won't let you down*, Tom thought. The three of them backed out of the stable until they were in the cool air outside.

As Jacob closed the door and locked it, he whispered. "I think I know the way to Ravira."

"Show us," said Tom.

Jacob's face twist into a frown as he glanced at Silver. "We should leave him here," he said. "Otherwise, the village patrols will probably kill him."

"But he's on our side!" Elenna protested.

"They're afraid of anything that looks like a Hound," said Jacob. "Your horse should stay, too."

Tom didn't like the idea of leaving his companions, but if he couldn't be with his father, then he'd rather someone stayed behind with him. He glanced at Elenna, but couldn't read her expression in the gloom.

"If there's more than one of these Hounds where we're going," he said, "we might struggle to protect them."

His friend nodded, and crouching beside Silver, whispered to him that she needed him to stay put and guard Taladon. Silver barked in understanding. Tom looped Storm's reins over a post, and ruffled his mane. "If my father comes round," he said. "At least he'll know we're nearby."

Storm whickered softly and nuzzled Tom's shoulder.

"I almost forgot," said Jacob, darting quickly along the edge of the stable. He came back holding a sword and belt. Tom recognised the engraved hilt at once.

"My father's sword!"

"We took it from him after he was bitten," said Jacob.

Tom drew the blade, which

glistened in the moonlight, then
sheathed it again, and offered it to
Elenna. "You should take this," he
said.

Elenna took a step back in shock.
"I... I can't. It belongs to a Master of
the Beasts."

The rattle of chains and a snarl
sounded from within the barn.

"Please," Tom insisted. "He has no
use for it at the moment."

Elenna took the belt and fastened it

in place, then gripped the hilt. "I can feel its power," she said.

"It may be all that stands in the way of evil," Tom replied.

The three of them made their way towards the centre of Shrayton.

"I don't understand," said Tom. "Taladon's an experienced fighter. How did one of these Hounds even get close to him?"

Jacob unhitched a gate to let them through. "He went to help a farmer who'd been bitten, but the next we heard the warrior himself had been attacked. The men wanted to kill him straightaway, but he persuaded them to lock him up instead. The oddest thing was that a strange light appeared in the stables just after we'd left him."

Tom glanced across at Elenna, as

Jacob led them through the outskirts of the village, which was made up of simple huts. Some were boarded up with planks. "That light must have been Aduro," he whispered, then louder to Jacob, "Where are you taking us?"

Jacob paused behind a larger building that must have been the village hall. "The well in the main square," said the boy in a hushed voice. "The strangeness started when the well dried up. We heard these eerie, echoing howls – they seemed to be coming from the well itself!"

Tom remembered his father's last words: *It's deep...*

"It sounds like Ravira's lurking down there, whatever type of Beast it is," said Elenna.

"This way," said Jacob, pointing. As

they rounded the edge of the building, he suddenly pressed himself back against the wall and put a finger to his lips. Shouts of "I saw something!" drifted through the air nearby.

Tom, with his hands on the wall, peered out and saw a crowd of a dozen or so villagers, all wielding flaming torches and makeshift weapons. They were heading straight for them.

CHAPTER THREE

INTO THE DARKNESS

Tom pressed himself against the wall,
and signalled for the others to do the
same. His heart thudded as the
footsteps drew closer.

"Was it a Hound?" one of the
villagers shouted.

It's a good job we left Silver behind,
Tom thought.

"I don't know," called another. "It

looked like more than one."

The crowd passed a few paces from where Tom, Elenna and the boy were hiding in the shadows. Tom heard Jacob's foot scuff the ground, and the hindmost member of the patrol party spun around. Tom pushed Jacob's head down as he and Elenna ducked. He held his breath, expecting to be set upon at any moment.

"I think I saw something over there," said one of the villagers. Tom peered over the edge of the fence and saw a man pointing with his pitchfork in the opposite direction.

"That was close," whispered Elenna, as the footsteps and the flickering torchlight moved away.

"We're near to the well," said Jacob. "Come on."

But as soon as they'd taken a few

more steps, they heard a cry of alarm.
A boy, no older than Tom himself,
shot past like a pale spectre in the
dark. Jacob pushed Tom into the
narrow pathway between two
buildings as the rest of the mob
thundered past, fire swooping from
their torches. "Catch him!" a man
shouted. "He's one of them, for sure!"

Tom could only watch as the lead
villager threw a rope weighted at
both ends with stones. It wrapped
itself around the boy's legs, and he
sprawled across the ground. The
crowd surrounded him in a second,
and levelled their weapons.

Tom started to move from the
darkness, his hand on the hilt of his
sword, but Jacob gripped his
shoulder. "Wait!" he hissed.

"Please!" cried the boy. "It's me,

Evan. I've not been bitten."

"Check him," said the man who'd brought him down. "Stay away from his teeth!"

A man clutching an axe crouched and gripped the boy's arm. He inspected it, then the other, before lifting up his shirt. "He's telling the truth. Sorry, Evan. We had to be sure."

The mob stepped away, and the man with the axe offered the boy a hand to get up.

"You shouldn't have run," he said.

"Now, get yourself a weapon and follow us. Anything will do. There's safety in numbers."

The boy brushed himself down, and slowly the mob moved off through the village.

Tom felt a burst of panic. "If their search takes them to the old stables..." he muttered.

"Storm and Fleetfoot are there with your father," said Elenna, putting a hand on his arm.

"What if they get scared by the fire?" Tom said. "And what about Silver?"

Tom felt torn. *Maybe I should go back?* he thought. *But if I do, there's no one to face Ravira.*

"The well's nearby," said Jacob.

Tom decided. "Ravira's the key. If we can't defeat her..." He was going

47

to say his father was as good as dead, but the words lodged in his throat. "We have to defeat her. Come on!"

They stayed as close to buildings as they could, moving in a low crouch. From across the village, they heard the distant shouts of the village patrol: "This way!" and "No, over here!", but otherwise the night was still and silent as a grave.

The well had been dug in the centre of the village square. The wide space seemed abandoned. Tom led the way over to the waist-high wall of the well, scanning the surrounding buildings for any sign of danger. Shadows clung to every surface, but nothing stirred. Above the well was a rusty winding mechanism, and empty buckets littered the ground. Only a short length of rope, frayed at the end, wound around the spindle.

"It hasn't been used in ages," Jacob explained.

Peering into the black abyss, Tom's nostrils filled with the stench of stagnant air. He picked up a rock from the ground and dropped it. He half-expected to hear a distant *plop*, but all that echoed back was a chilling silence. There was a slight draft of heat on his face. The metal above creaked.

"Can you feel that?" he said to Elenna, holding his palm out over the top of the well. His friend did the same, and nodded.

"Heat," she said. "There's definitely something down there."

Ravira! Tom thought, grimly.

"How will you get down without a rope?" asked Jacob.

Tom scanned the well again. "It's narrow enough for us to climb down. We can press our backs across one wall, our feet against the other."

A flicker of fear crossed Elenna's face, but she set her jaw hard.

Tom knew his friend was afraid of heights – but he also knew she was brave.

"No problem," she whispered.

As Tom started to climb onto the rim, Jacob shook his head. "I... I can't go with you. It's just..."

Tom paused. "It's all right," he said. "I don't expect you to come. It's not your father who's in danger." Even in the darkness, Tom saw Jacob's face flush.

"It's not that," said the boy. "You see, my father *has* been bitten. He was the farmer who your father went to help. I'm sorry. I didn't want to say before. Bo's his name. He's a tall man, with a scar on his cheek... If you find him...do what you can."

"We'll do our best to save him," said Tom.

Elenna joined Tom at the edge of the well. "Goodbye, Jacob," she said.

Tom went first, lowering himself carefully, lodging his legs against one side and his back against the other. He had to strap his shield across his front, and his sword sheath clanked against the stone. Elenna came next, clutching her quiver and bow to her chest. As she scraped down after him, flakes of old stone and moss pattered on Tom's head.

"Take it steady," he said. "If we fall, my shield may not be enough to stop us."

It was slow going, but as the fading

light from above shrank away, the heat from below grew stronger. Once or twice, Tom thought he saw light far below, a dim yellow glow. In the confines of the circular walls, he could hear Elenna's heaving breath. His legs were starting to tire from the descent, and grazes on his back made him grit his teeth. *Just how deep is this well?* he asked himself.

Suddenly Elenna cried out in panic. Tom heard something like a crack above, and a jagged piece of stone tumbled past as he looked up.

Elenna's body smashed into his legs, wrenching his grip on the wall. They both plummeted in the darkness.

Tom reached for the walls to slow himself, but his fingertips scraped on the rough stone. His leg snagged on the other side of the well and he toppled over, his head cracking against brickwork. A moment later his back slammed into something soft, and the air burst from his lungs. He heard Elenna groan beside him.

Tom's vision cleared and he realised he was sliding down a muddy incline on his front, and spinning in circles. He caught sight of Elenna tumbling after him, then the view revolved to a sight more terrifying. Waiting for them at the bottom of the slope was a bubbling orange pool that glowed with fiery danger. *A lake of lava!*

CHAPTER FOUR

BOATMAN BO

Tom managed to draw his sword, and tried to stab it into the ground to halt the movement of his body. He wasn't strong enough and kept on sliding. He tried again and managed to sink the point of the blade into the mud. He leant against the hilt with his shoulder to slow himself, and came to a halt. Elenna rushed towards him on her back, so he reached out.

"Your hand!" he shouted.

Elenna threw out her arm as she slid past, and Tom gripped her sleeve, taking the strain on the hilt of his sword. She jolted to a stop beside him. He was glad to see her eyes were open, if a little wide with panic. A moment later, her bow and quiver slid down the slope too, and fell into her hand.

"Use your sword like this," he said.

Elenna drew Taladon's blade and buried it in the ground as Tom had. They pulled themselves to their feet and looked around.

The lake of molten rock bubbled and spat, shifting with hot currents. The black walls of a gigantic cavern rose on either side, and sharp stalactites like rotten teeth jutted from the roof. Tom looked back the way they'd fallen, and saw a rough hole where the bottom of the well opened onto the tunnel. It was too high off the ground for them to climb back in. The temperature was higher than ever, and seemed to press up from below like some sort of breathing creature. Flickering orange light played over Elenna's glistening face and sweat trickled down Tom's back.

"How can this place even exist?"

said Elenna. "Aduro never mentioned it."

"Perhaps he didn't even know it was here," said Tom. He shared his friend's surprise. *I thought Avantia had no more secrets…*

"The only way is down," said Elenna.

"I bet that's where Ravira waits," Tom said.

Using their swords to lean on, they took careful steps down towards the lake of lava. The smell of sulphur thickened in the air, and Tom realised that the mud he trudged through, and which covered his clothes, was damp ash.

With the heat baking their faces, they stopped a few paces short of the lake edge, where the slope levelled off a little.

"What now?" asked Elenna,
sheathing Taladon's sword.

Tom scanned up and down the
bank. A sliver of white caught his eye
to the left.

"This way," he pointed.

As they trudged through the ash,
the cavern loomed above them and
the lava seemed to sizzle and hiss as

though speaking in some evil tongue. *This is Ravira's home*, Tom realised.

They came to a stone walkway rising above the licking flames of the lake. It had been constructed from some polished white rock like marble, and snaked off across the lava, fading to nothing but a dim glow in the gloom.

"It must lead to Ravira," said Tom, taking a step onto the stone to test it.

"Are you sure?" asked Elenna. "What if it's a trap?"

Tom hesitated, and looked back to his friend. "I don't think we have a choice."

He drew his sword and brought his other foot onto the stone. Elenna nodded, and followed. Together, with the molten lava lapping just a pace on either side, they walked the white path. Above, the cavernous roof arched beyond the dark swirls of smoke. The stone path seemed never-ending. Tom felt the heat rise through the soles of his shoes, and the hot air drew beads of sweat from his brow.

"It's like the Stonewin volcano," he said to Elenna, thinking of the home of Epos the Flame Bird. But the air here was laced with dread. What sort of awful Beast could live in these conditions?

He heard Elenna's footsteps following. When he turned, he couldn't even see the bank they'd left behind! But when he looked ahead again, his fear doubled, and he swallowed. The path they were walking along sank slowly beneath the surface of the lava.

"It's moving!" he gasped.

Elenna shrank towards Tom as the white stone vanished from sight, leaving them exposed on an island just large enough for them to stand on. "I knew it," she said. "It's a trap!"

Tom looked hopelessly in every direction, looking for a way to escape. He even looked up to the roof of the cavern, but it was many feet high.

"Not a trap," called a droning voice.

"Just a way to prevent unwelcome guests."

Tom and Elenna turned to see a flat-bottomed boat drifting towards them across the lake. The lava lapped at the sides, spitting golden sparks. The craft seemed to be made of wood. *It can't possibly be…* thought Tom, staring at the boat. The polished hull cleaved through the bubbling lava, reflecting the red glow.

A figure dressed from head to toe in

a dark cloak, and wearing a wide hood, pushed the boat with even strokes with what looked like a wooden pole. As he drifted towards them, Tom swung his shield in front of him.

"Who are you?" he demanded.

The figure, standing at the rear of the boat, gave a flick of the pole, and the magical craft drifted to a halt beside their tiny island.

"I am the boatman," he snarled. "What is your business here?"

Tom thought fast. *The wrong answer and we'll have no chance of crossing the lava,* he realised.

"We wish to join Ravira's Hounds," he said.

"Only those who have been bitten may cross to the Queen's city," said the boatman. "Say farewell to your lives."

The ground beneath Tom's feet began to sink, and the lava lapped higher, sizzling against the white stone.

Tom shot a glance at Elenna and quickly pushed the point of his sword into the skin of his lower leg twice, clenching his teeth against the stinging pain. Elenna understood and did the same.

"The Hounds have tasted our blood," said Tom, sheathing his sword and tugging up his trouser leg to show the fake teeth-marks.

The ground stopped moving. With his free hand, the boatman pulled down the hood, revealing a bald head, mottled red with the heat of the lava. Sweat slicked his face, and down one cheek Tom saw a pale scar. But his eyes drew Tom's attention most of all. They were coated with a milky layer and stared unblinking.

"You're Jacob's father!" gasped Elenna.

The man's dark eyes flickered in recognition at the sound of the boy's name. *He's under Ravira's enchantment,*

Tom thought, *but there's still good inside him.*

"Jacob…" said the boatman, his pale eyes softening. "Is he…?" His face hardened again. "I am boatman to Ravira now," he said. "I shall take you to her."

CHAPTER FIVE

THE UNDERWORLD CITY

The Boatman dropped the pole and shot out both hands, gripping Tom and Elenna by their necks. His fingers felt cold, despite the heat of the place and he yanked them off the island. Tom yelled as his feet almost slipped into the lava, then tipped forwards, sprawling into the bottom of the boat.

He glanced at Elenna lying beside him, pale with shock, then pushed himself up onto his elbows. The boatman poled the boat away from the tiny island of white stone. *We're going deeper into the Underworld of Avantia than ever before*, Tom thought. *Will we ever see the outside world again?*

With smooth strokes, Jacob's father guided the boat through the lava lake. He paid no attention to his two passengers.

"Why hasn't he changed into a hound?" whispered Elenna.

Tom shrugged. "Perhaps because Ravira needed him for this," he said. "Or maybe it's because the moon is not yet at its fullest."

The lake narrowed into a river, with black banks on either side, swallowed up in darkness. Tom saw shifting shadows, and once or twice thought he caught flashes of pale light at the edge of his vision. *Not lava...* But whenever he turned to look, they were gone.

"I don't think we're alone," he said to Elenna.

He leant over the edge of the boat, and peered into the swirling currents of molten rock. How deep did it go?

A tongue of flame leapt from the lava, making him jerk backwards. Elenna caught his arm and the boat rocked as more flames soared up on each side. Soon the boat was surrounded with a curtain of flickering fire. The heat singed his hair and eyebrows, almost unbearably hot against his skin.

"Someone doesn't want us to pass," said Elenna.

Bo the boatman stalled the boat.
"I don't understand. This has never
happened before."

Ravira must have sensed our presence,
Tom thought. He didn't like doing it,
but he drew his sword and pointed it
at Jacob's father. "Keep going."

The boatman paused for a moment,
then nodded. "If you insist, but my
mistress's anger will be great."

"Let me handle your mistress,"
said Tom.

The boatman resumed with steady strokes, taking them through the wall of fire. Flames licked along the edges of the boat, leaping up to head height.

"Duck!" shouted Tom.

Arcs of lava lashed the air over the craft. Mysteriously, the boatman remained untouched. A sound like thunder echoed through the cavern, followed by a chorus of distant howls.

The boatman left the violent flames behind and rounded a curve in the river. Tom and Elenna gasped together as the vista opened up before them.

Looming high over another bank was an entire city made of white stone.

Tall battlements protected a raised fortress in the distance, but hundreds of buildings littered the lower slopes,

with dusty tracks leading between
them. The stone here was slightly
different, glittering with crystals.

"It's like another city!" said Elenna.

"Ruled over by a Beast," growled
Tom. He stabbed his sword towards
the shore. "Take us in, boatman."

Jacob's father obeyed, and with
a single swish of his pole, the boat
slid into the shallows and butted up
against the bank. Tom leapt out onto
dry land, and Elenna jumped after

him. "It's good to be off that lake of fire!" she said.

Tom felt the heat of the ground more than ever through the soles of his boots, and a trail of smoke drifted up. *I'm not so sure we're any safer here*, Tom thought. *Ravira's magic rules this place, on the land as well as the lake.*

"Be careful," whispered the boatman, and Tom couldn't tell if the words were a threat or a warning.

"Your son misses you, Bo," he said.

The boatman lifted his head a fraction, and even under the hood, Tom thought he saw the man's lips curl into a smile. Then it slipped away. "Ravira's Hounds will tear you to pieces," he said, pushing the boat back out into the lake.

Tom and Elenna turned to face the Underworld city.

"This is Ravira's lair," said Tom. "Keep your eyes open."

Elenna sheathed Taladon's sword and instead put an arrow to her bowstring. "I feel better with this," she explained. As they walked up one of the glowing white paths, she kept the bow lowered, but ready.

Silence hung between the buildings. Tom led the way through the deserted streets towards the fortress. The buildings here had smooth edges, almost as if they'd been carved from the ground and worn smooth. Instead of windows and doors there were dark holes that swallowed up the meagre light. There were no signs of life anywhere.

"Do you think anyone ever lived down here?" Elenna whispered.

"If they did," muttered Tom, gripping his sword tighter, "it was deserted a long time ago."

But at least one person lives down here. A Beast, anyway…

He lost track of the turns they'd taken, but all the time the fortress walls loomed taller ahead. They climbed a curving street until they reached a wide, open archway in the outer walls. "No turning back now," said Tom.

A low growl made the breath catch

in his throat. He backed away, and pulled Elenna through the low doorway of the nearest abandoned building.

"What's wrong?" she hissed.

Tom put his finger to his lips, and stared out of the window. His heart knocked and his mouth went dry.

From somewhere to the right, he heard the soft padding of paws. He slowly manoeuvred his shield up.

A shadow fell into view five paces ahead, and a cloud of vapour drifted past. Elenna lifted her bow and pulled back the string. The shadow shifted and a creature stalked into view.

A Hound of Avantia!

It looked like a hunting dog, strong, with thin dark fur. The vapour Tom had seen seeped from its long

muzzle, and black lips twitched above dagger-like teeth. The Hound's eyes were the rubiest of reds, giving it a hot, deadly stare.

Just like in Aduro's vision, thought Tom.

The Hound paused by the window, and lifted its snout, sniffing the air.

Tom kept still, not daring to breath. He was sure the creature couldn't see them in the dark interior, but how good was its sense of smell?

After what seemed like an age, the Hound paced on with a low, menacing growl, the powerful muscles of its shoulders bulging as it patrolled the buildings of the white city.

Just as it was about to round a corner further along the street, Elenna levelled an arrow out of the window at its back.

"No!" hissed Tom, pushing the point down. "That Hound used to be a citizen of Avantia."

Elenna relaxed her hold on the bow, and flushed with shame.

"I'm sorry – I'd forgotten."

"That's all right," said Tom. "Did

you see its eyes – there was an
intelligence there that was almost
human. And until Ravira's gone, that
poor person is trapped. Just like my
father."

They crept out of the building and
back towards the archway. It, like
everything else, seemed chiselled
from a solid piece of stone, rather
than blocks as in Hugo's Palace.

They moved into the palace
courtyard. It was darker here, as if
the stone had sucked up all the light.
A huge stalactite stabbed down from
the roof, its point ending a few feet
above the ground. The air seemed
dense with the smell of animals, like
a stables or kennels. As they pressed
on, weapons ready, Tom's eyes

adjusted to the gloom. They rounded the stalactite, and he saw a staircase, with wide, stone steps, rising straight ahead. His eyes followed it upwards until they reached a huge throne, where a statue sat half-clothed in darkness.

The statue shifted.

"Ravira!" challenged Tom.

A woman's voice like whispering leaves drifted down.

"Welcome to the Underworld, child of Taladon!"

CHAPTER SIX

MISTRESS OF THE HOUNDS

As Ravira spoke, a grinding sound filled the courtyard, and the throne moved forwards by some hidden mechanism. Tom swallowed with dread as a shaft of moonlight fell on the seat's occupant from above. The woman – if he could call the Beast that – was at least seven feet tall, and wrapped in a filthy pale shroud that was spattered with dried blood and

torn away in patches to reveal green-tinged flesh beneath. Her face was almost human, but too long, as though it had been stretched and distorted. Her mouth hung open to reveal gums and jagged, cruel teeth. Her eyes blazed yellow as flaming torches, and white hair hung in matted strands to her shoulders.

Elenna pointed her arrow. "You've lost, Ravira!"

The Beast reached for the arms of her throne with long, grey fingers, and she stood up. Tom heard a rattle of metal, and saw with horror that two leather thongs hooked onto barbs seared into Ravira's palms. The skin puckered and stretched as they grew taut, and Ravira's thin lips stretched into a hideous smile.

"You're wrong," she snarled.

Around the base of the steps, six pairs of eyes blinked open, and six Hounds clambered to their feet. They gave a chorus of growls, drool trailing from their jaws.

Tom held his shield up, and adjusted his sword grip. Could they take on six of these creatures without killing them?

"Soon I will hold all Avantia on my leash," Ravira cackled. She tipped her head up into the shaft of light, and moved her face from side to side, bathing in the glow.

Tom realised that the light pierced through the cavern's roof. *She draws power from the moonlight*, Tom thought, remembering what Aduro had said back at the palace: *By the light of the moon, Taladon will change.*

"How *is* your father, Tom?" asked

Ravira, as though she had read his thoughts.

"Come down here and face me," said Tom.

Ravira laughed, a cracked and bitter sound. "My Hounds need to be fed, first," she said.

Lowering her right arm, she flicked the leashes, and three of the Hounds strained forward, eyes narrowed into ugly grimaces.

"We can do this," Tom whispered to Elenna. "We just need to get her out of the moonlight. If we can do that, the Beast will be weakened."

"I'm ready," she replied in low tones. "Let's distract the Hounds."

"Good plan!" said Tom. With a defiant yell, he charged at the dogs. He slashed his sword from side to side, and the Hounds reared back. He heard an arrow whish from Elenna's bow, but another hound leapt into the air and snatched the shaft mid-flight with a vicious growl.

"Try again!" shouted Tom, stabbing at one Hound, and smacking another across the muzzle with the flat of his blade. It stood at the base of the steps, head lowered and growling – but it did not attack.

That's right, thought Tom. *Play it*

smart – or next time, you'll get worse.

Elenna's bow twanged, and another Hound sprang up on its powerful hind-legs. The arrow deflected off its hide, clattering uselessly into the steps.

The dog gave a triumphant howl, and stalked towards Elenna as she desperately tried to string another arrow. Tom left off his attack and slammed into the Hound's flank, sending it rolling into two of its pack.

Ravira hissed above and yanked back, pulling on all the leashes, and coiling them around her wrists.

Her Hounds gathered at the base of the steps to form a wall of solid flesh between Tom and Ravira. They snapped and snarled.

"We can't risk fighting them," said Elenna. "One bite, and we'll go the same way as your father."

Tom knew his friend was right. "Let's retreat," he said.

"Yes!" called Ravira, fixing them with a mocking, triumphant gaze. "My Hounds like their prey to run. Fear will make your blood all the sweeter!" She slackened the chains a little, and the dogs surged forward, straining at their leashes. "I'll even give you a chance to save your lives," she said. "How does three heartbeats sound?"

"What does she mean?" asked Elenna.

Tom felt his heart thumping. Once... Twice... It meant that on the third beat...

"We run!" he shouted.

CHAPTER SEVEN

THE HUNT

Tom grabbed Elenna's hand and they raced back towards the arch.

"After them!" Ravira screeched to her dogs.

Tom heard the rattle of chains as the Hounds pursued them. With a grinding sound, a stone portcullis descended swiftly from the top of the arch. He couldn't see how the mechanism of the gate worked.

Ravira's magic must be controlling it! he thought.

"Quickly!" he shouted to Elenna. "Or we'll be trapped!"

He threw himself forward, rolling across the ground with Elenna at his side. Only when he turned back did he see his shield on the other side. It must have slipped off his shoulder.

Tom quickly snatched it back, just as the portcullis slammed down, brushing his fingertips. The pack of Hounds slid up short on the other side. They leapt at the portcullis with their front paws, sticking their drooling fangs through the gaps.

"Keep running!" cackled Ravira. "Your lives are mine!"

The gate began to creak open again. The Hounds barked even louder, their eyes gleaming with intelligence.

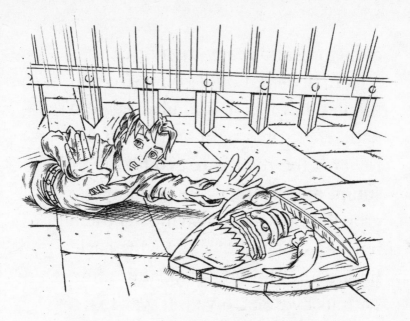

Tom turned and looked frantically
into the strange white city.

"Come on!"

They sprinted back towards the
buildings, slipping into one of the
many streets leading to the river of
lava. As they plunged within the
maze of paths, he heard the Hounds
coming after them.

"Which way?" cried Elenna.

A Hound leapt out in front of them,

crouching and ready to attack.

Elenna veered off down a street to the left, but the Hound blocked Tom's path. He turned right and ran back towards the river, pursued by the sound of scraping claws and low growling. He hated leaving his friend, but he had no choice. Looking back he saw the Hound racing after him with its eyes narrowed. It was so much quicker than Tom: it wouldn't be long before it caught him.

Tom charged towards the river's edge. He felt the creature's teeth snatch at the back of his tunic, and tugged himself free with a tearing sound. At any moment he expected to feel the vicious jaws sink into his neck.

As he reached the bank, the heat baking his face, he skidded sideways.

The Hound couldn't stop, and slid past, snarling in terror as it approached the bubbling stream. One paw went over the edge, touching the molten rock, and the Hound howled in agony as smoke rose from its scorched fur and flesh. Tom felt a pang of sympathy as the creature rolled on the bank.

Then he heard a scream. *Elenna!*

Tom left the injured Hound and ran

back up the hill, drawing his sword.

"Elenna!" he shouted. "Where are you?"

She called again. "Help! Tom!"

Tom followed the sound, and came across a terrible sight. In a small square, two Hounds faced his friend.

She was pressed up against a wall, and the creatures stood just a few paces away, heads lowered and backs hunched, ready to attack. Elenna had

an arrow strung to her bow, and was pointing it desperately, first at one Hound, then the other.

If she shoots one, the other will attack, Tom realised. *I need to distract them.*

The Hounds growled and snapped, edging forward. Over the buildings Tom heard Ravira's cackle.

"Injure one!" Tom yelled. "It's the only way."

At the sound of his voice, both creatures snapped their heads in his direction.

Elenna let loose an arrow into the hind leg of the one on the left, making it crumple to its side. Tom ran at the other, smashing his shield across its muzzle. The Hound backed away, growling with frustration.

Tom and Elenna darted between them and ran on through the streets.

Tom kept his eye on the fortress. "We can't run forever," he said. "We'll collapse or be bitten. We have to tackle Ravira."

Elenna nodded, but they heard barking behind them. Two more Hounds slunk into view twenty paces away, their eyes flashing with malice.

Elenna gripped Tom's arm, and pointed to a tall turret at one corner of the fortress. "It's a watchtower of some sort," she said. "If we climb up, they won't be able to follow."

"Good thinking!" said Tom.

They ran, with the Hounds on their heels, and threw themselves against the wall. The stone was rough enough to find handholds. Tom just managed to pull his foot out of reach as one of the Hounds leapt at the tower, teeth snatching at the empty air.

"Go higher!" Elenna yelled.

Reaching up, and placing his feet carefully on the narrow ledges, Tom climbed until he was sure they were safe. Looking down, he saw that two more Hounds had joined the others, and the four creatures made a writhing, angry pack. He felt his heart slow a little. The walls of the fortress were still a long way up, but he thought they could make it to the top.

We're safe, for a while at least.

One of the Hounds opened its jaws wide and sank its teeth into the stone, scattering chips of debris. The tower seemed to vibrate slightly.

"No normal dog could do that!" Elenna gasped.

A second Hound jumped at the wall and bit out a chunk of masonry the size of Tom's head.

"These aren't normal dogs," he replied. The other Hounds joined the feeding frenzy and the tower shuddered. "We don't have long. We need to get to the top before—"

A crumbling sound cut him off, as

a cloud of stones fell away from the bottom of the tower. Slowly at first, the structure began to lean. The Hounds scattered from the base, howling in triumph. Tom could do nothing as the whole world seemed to tip.

With his fingers still desperately gripping the wall, the ground rushed towards him.

This is it, was his last thought. *Today is the day I die.*

STORY TWO

The moon is full. I feel its power over me as its milky light floods the stable. I do not know whether to howl like a Hound or stand up to Ravira like a man. Her poison flows in my veins and it is all I can do to resist the snarls that rise up in my chest. I struggle to take control and yank at the chains holding me to this wall. At last the stones give. I'm free!

But no. Ravira calls me, as she calls all her Hounds. I feel her spirit take over completely. I am man no more, never to wear The Golden Armour again.

Must go... Must run... The time has come to take my place at my mistress's side. Out there a whole kingdom waits. We'll sink our teeth into them while they sleep.

Soon Ravira will reign over all.

Ravira's faithful servant,

Taladon

CHAPTER ONE

AT THE MERCY OF THE BEAST

Tom hit the ground so hard the wind was knocked out of him. Dust filled his eyes and throat, and rocks smashed into his limbs from every side, crushing him against the ground. He thought he heard Elenna scream, but in the barrage of thuds and cracks he couldn't be sure. The weight above him pressed down

harder all the time, until he was sure
his bones would be ground to dust.

Then quiet settled. He opened his
eyes, and all was dark. *I'm alive!*
Almost as soon this thought sparked,
panic spread into his heart. *Elenna!*

He called out her name. His voice
sounded muffled in his coffin of
fallen stone. No answer. "Elenna!" he
shouted again. He thought he heard
a whimper, or a groan. He called
a third time, his voice now hoarse.
This time his ears definitely picked up

a sound. *So she was alive, and conscious. But how badly was she hurt?* He tried to move, but other than clenching one fist, the rest of his limbs seemed locked in place.

Tom tried to quench his rising terror, but it kept flooding up. *We're trapped! The air down here won't last for long. And when it does run out, we'll slowly suffocate. If we don't get out, there will be no one to stop Ravira. And my father will remain a Hound forever. Avantia will be doomed!*

Above, he heard the trickle of pebbles. He guessed that the debris was settling.

"Don't worry, Elenna!" he shouted. "I'll think of something!"

Tom tried to move his limbs, but every part of him seemed locked in place. He just managed to turn his head to one side.

The rocks shifted again, and this time there were definitely other sounds above. He felt the weight on his chest lessen a little. *Perhaps Elenna's up there!*

A shaft of light appeared through a crack between the fallen stones.

"Elenna?" he called. "Down here!"

More light. More sounds.

But then Tom smelled the hot stink of animal. It could only mean one thing.

"No!" he heard Elenna whimper.

He tried to reach for his sword, not caring about the skin that scraped off his knuckles. He found the hilt, just as a huge stone slab lifted away. He came face to face with one of Ravira's Hounds. Its lips curled back over sharp incisors, and a trickle of drool

dripped onto his cheek. Tom yanked
his sword free, but the Hound
snapped its teeth over his forearm.
Tom cried out as the fangs sank
through his skin, digging into
his flesh.

I've been bitten!

Almost at once, he felt a surge
through his blood. It spread from his
arm, across his chest and down

through his body, right to the tips of his toes.

The Hound released him, and Tom saw puncture marks on his arm: deep gashes, but not bleeding heavily. The dog's eyes shimmered with evil triumph. Tom sank back, as more Hounds appeared above him, pawing away the remaining stones. One leant towards his face with gaping jaws, but then gripped the collar of his tunic instead.

The monster dragged him from the rubble. Dust caked Tom's sweating skin, and he tasted the grit between his teeth.

"Tom?" said Elenna.

Tom saw his friend held by another of the Hounds. Her clothes were torn and bloody, and her face was covered in white dust, and a nasty scrape across her cheekbone.

"Anything broken?" he asked.

She shook her head weakly.
"I don't think so."

"Have you been…?" he began.

His glance followed her eyes
towards her leg. There, just above
her knee beside Taladon's sword,
Tom saw the same teeth marks
through her trousers.

"I feel different," said Elenna.

"It's not hot anymore."

A sense of dread seeped through Tom's blood, and he realised that he couldn't feel the intense heat from the lava either.

How long do we have? he wondered. *There's only one way to save ourselves now. To save everyone. We have to defeat Ravira.*

The Hounds dragged them away from the fallen tower and back into the fortress through the gap in the collapsed wall.

"Don't fight them," said Tom. "They may be our only way back to their mistress."

The two dogs stalked through a gloomy vaulted passage, holding Tom and Elenna so that their feet brushed through thin air above the ground.

The animals smelled like meat left

in the sun and their powerful lungs made their ribcages swell with each breath. The other two Hounds padded menacingly ahead, occasionally turning their massive heads to look at the captives.

Tom felt the strange thrill through his blood again – making him shiver. Taladon had changed by the light of the moon. Would they do so, too?

The Hound dragging him suddenly quickened its steps and released Tom, throwing him across the ground. Tom sprang up, bruised and battered, and lifted his shield across his front. Elenna climbed to her feet more gingerly, as the Hounds retreated. They stood at the edge of a dark, semi-circular chamber, with a raised platform at one end approached by a wide set of stairs. Through arrow

slits in one wall, the faint glow of the
lava river cast orange shadows across
the roof. A single column of
moonlight shone from the ceiling
onto Ravira's throne.

The Mistress of the Underworld
leaned forward, her shroud swishing
around her hunched shoulders and
strands of white hair streaming in the

warm breeze. She pointed a long
bony finger at Tom and Elenna, and
raised her sickly face defiantly.
Sucking in a hissing breath, her eyes
blazed the same colour as the lava.

"Welcome back, *my* children!"

CHAPTER TWO

OLD FRIENDS, NEW ENEMIES

As her laughter died, she raised her
hands. Tom saw that she now held
several leashes. At the same time,
more shafts of moonlight broke
through the ceiling, casting silvered
rays over the chamber walls. A row
of Hounds stood waiting beneath her
throne, teeth bared and sides
heaving. Tom counted at least

a dozen. Each had a collar from which a leash trailed through a ring above their heads on the wall to Ravira's hands. Tom felt pinned in place, skewered by their blue glare.

"Meet your brothers and sisters," said Ravira.

"There are more than before," whispered Elenna.

"That's because more people are being bitten all the time," Tom replied. "If we can't stop Ravira, all Avantia will follow."

He drew his sword, and levelled its tip at Ravira's sagging, haggard face. "While there's blood in my veins, I'll never be one of them," he shouted.

A sickly grin spread across her scarlet gums. "Don't you see?" she said. "The blood in your veins is already poisoned. There's nothing you can do to stop it."

She waved her hands to the side. Tom heard a sound in the roof of the chamber, and looked up. The shadows shifted, and suddenly he was blinded. With a cry, he shielded his eyes and dropped to his knees, hearing Elenna moan as well. Around him, a disc of pale light shone on the stone floor. *Moonlight!*

His eyes adjusted but the light seemed to burn his skin like a thousand pinpricks. Next to him,

Elenna was writhing in pain. Around the room's edge, Ravira's pets took up a pitiful howling.

"What's happening?" Tom gasped.

"That was just a little taste of what is to come," said Ravira, waving her hand. As she did so, the moonlight over Tom died again. He stabbed his sword into the ground and climbed to his feet. He helped Elenna up, and noticed that her skin seemed paler than before. He peered at the back of his hand. The flesh seemed almost white. Elenna caught the panicked look in his eyes.

"Can it happen so fast?" she asked.

"Ravira's toying with us," he said grimly. "Soon we'll really start to change, like Taladon."

The Hounds snarled, the hair on their backs bristling, and rancid drool falling from their muzzles.

With a scraping sound, the wall beside Ravira's throne scraped backwards. Tom saw two more dogs. *She's growing more powerful all the time*, he thought. But as the Hounds entered the chamber, he saw that both were limping, one with a folded forepaw, the other hobbling with an arrow protruding from its hind leg.

"They're the Hounds we injured," he said.

"Come, my brave beauties," Ravira called. "Take your places."

The Hounds made their way to the edge of the chamber, and stood under the columns of moonlight beside the other members of their pack. Almost at once, Tom saw the arrow disintegrate to nothing, and the charred paw become whole

127

again. *They're practically invincible!*

There had to be a way to reach Ravira. He remembered how Aduro had described her: *a cursed Beast.* If Ravira was under some evil enchantment, perhaps he could reason with her. Tom sheathed his sword and stepped towards the Beast. The Hound growled.

"Another step, and your friend will be picking scraps of you from the ground," said the Beast Mistress.

"Why are you doing this?" Tom asked. "You weren't always evil, were you?" Ravira blinked and then her eyes widened slightly. "You don't have to do this!" Tom continued.

Her face twisted in a grimace. "Silence!" she hissed, furiously lunging for him.

As she took herself out of the

moonlight, Tom noticed a change. He thought he saw her features soften and her hair thicken, taking on a dark hue. For a brief moment, he caught a glimpse of a younger woman, maybe not even a Beast at all. Ravira backed into the moonlight again. Her skin wrinkling like a rotting apple. "You know nothing of my curse!" she hissed.

Ravira twisted her hideous face into the moonlight, bathing in its glow. She snapped her hands, lashing the leashes and making her dogs writhe beside the wall.

"She needs the moon to survive in this form," Elenna whispered. "It's the source of all her power."

Perhaps while she isn't watching…

Drawing his sword with a flash of steel, Tom threw himself forward with a furious cry. He dodged the snapping jaws of a Hound and slashed downwards at one of the leashes. Ravira jerked it out of range, and another Hound pounced from the wall and planted its paws into his chest. It felt like being kicked by a horse and the force flung Tom back. He rolled across the floor, dazed, to Elenna's feet. He stood shakily, growling in anger. He lifted his sword over his head, and tried to attack again. Elenna caught his sword arm.

"Tom, no!" she shouted. She lowered her voice. "We can't defeat Ravira through anger. Can't you see?"

Ravira gave a hissing laugh. "No, little girl. If your friend wants to fight, let's see a fight." With a swish of her hand, the doorway beside the throne platform slid open. A massive

shadow filled the space, and two red
eyes gleamed. Moonlight caught the
flash of glistening white fangs. A
Hound, bulkier than the others,
loped into the chamber. Tom stared
into the eyes, recognising something
there which chilled his blood as cold
as a glacial stream.

"So much for the Master of the
Beasts," scoffed Ravira. "Tom, meet
your father."

CHAPTER THREE

ECLIPSE

The Hound snarled and stared at
Tom. A manacle was attached around
its forepaw and a piece of chain
trailed across the ground.

"Father?" Tom said.

The creature lunged. Tom lifted his
shield and braced himself as the
Hound's teeth raked across the
surface. He was knocked back with
the force of the attack, and only just

managed to stay on his feet. As Tom
looked over the rim, he saw the
monster sloping off, climbing the
steps up to Ravira's throne. *Is that
truly my father?* As the Hound loped
away, he turned to cast Tom one last
glance and as their eyes met he saw
a momentary light of recognition
there. *Yes, it really is him.*

"Release him!" Tom shouted at
Ravira.

"Don't worry," said the Beast with
a cackle. "Soon you'll join him at my

side, boy. Would you like a taste of the future?"

She made the same gesture as before with her hands, palms up, and the beams of moonlight shone down through the roof. Elenna clutched her middle and fell to her knees, groaning, and Tom felt burning across his skin and the puncture marks in his flesh glowed red. He fought to remain on his feet as an ache like nothing he'd ever known surged through his bones. The pain wasn't only physical. Anger rose in a dark tide, and hatred boiled in his heart.

I'm changing, he realised, *and there's nothing I can do.*

The moonlight dimmed and over his own moans Tom heard Ravira's laughter. "Do you feel it yet?" she asked. "The thirst for blood?"

Tom pointed his sword at her with a shaky arm. Ravira was right; he felt an incredibly strong urge to slay her. *I can't*, he told himself. *That's not what this is about*. "Come out of your moonlight and fight me," he said. "Or do you plan to stand up there like a coward?"

Ravira drew her chains towards her, and the Hounds yapped and growled. "I'm not a fool," she chided him. "For now, this place is my prison, but as my pack grows, I become more powerful. One day I will roam the upper world again. Avantia will be my kingdom."

"Never!" said Elenna.

As she shouted, Tom noticed something with horror.

"Elenna! Your teeth!"

His friend turned to him. Her

incisors seemed longer than before, and she ran her fingers along them, her face bone-white. Then her glance shifted to his hands. Tom looked and saw wispy pale hairs growing over the back of them. The fingers that gripped his sword hilt ended in long claw-like nails, thickened and yellowing. *It can't happen so soon*, he thought.

"It's time to join the pack," said Ravira. The moonlight shone again, and the pain returned. Elenna

collapsed into a ball but Tom stood
his ground. Pain came in bolts across
his chest and through his blurred
vision he saw the Hound that was his
father stalking towards him. Tom
held his sword out. The Hound
snapped and lunged but Tom
managed to hold it at bay. He could
feel anger inside him, and the sudden
desire for blood. He gritted his teeth,
fighting against the change.

*There has to be some way I can stop
this. Some way to stop the moonlight…*

A sudden memory flashed in his
brain: standing as a young boy in
Errinel, his Aunt and Uncle at his
side. They were watching as the
moon drifted in front of the sun,
blocking it out in the middle of the
day. He remembered the rim of
burning light around the dark disc

of the moon. An eclipse!

But eclipses came round once a generation. He couldn't hope for one now. Unless...

The Hound pounced, and Tom turned the blade to strike with the flat side. With a yowl, his enchanted father skulked off. Tom's sword dropped from his hand as another wave of pain exploded through his body. He felt his own teeth shifting in his jaws, growing sharper, longer. To his side, Elenna clutched her head in agony. He squeezed closed his eyes against the scorching light, but a snarl made them snap open.

Taladon approached again, his teeth bared and his eyes glowing with hatred. Tom reached for his sword, his anger dampening the pain. He had the sudden urge to drive the point into the Hound's throat.

"Don't hurt him," gasped Elenna. "Remember he's your father."

Tom felt a flush of shame. "I have to stop this before it's too late," he muttered. He searched the surface of his shield with his fingers until he found the dragon's scale. "Ferno," he said, speaking more strongly now. "If you can hear me, I need your help."

"No one can hear you!" roared Ravira.

Tom tried to stand, but fell back. It felt like some great weight was pinning him to the cold stone. "Soon it will all be over," said the Beast.

The moonlight suddenly dimmed and the weight lifted. Tom opened his eyes, and through the gap in the chamber roof, he saw the silhouette of a jagged wing, hovering high

overhead. "Ferno!" he called.

Staggering up, he pulled Elenna
to her feet. His friend's face had
changed, her jaw jutting out and her
eyes shifted further apart. "Elenna?"
he said. "Are you all right?"

She looked at him, and her eyes
widened. "Are *you* all right?"

A sudden hiss of fury made Tom
glance round at Ravira. Her head
jerked back and forth in panic as she
looked around the chamber. Shadows

were moving with the darting silhouette of Ferno above. Only a few shafts of moonlight remained, including the one that bathed Ravira.

"It's not enough!" said Elenna. "There's still a pillar of moonlight for her to stand in."

One Beast won't do it, Tom thought. *I need Epos too!*

"What's happening?" Ravira cried. "Hounds! Attack them!"

The pack surged forward from the wall, jaws slavering.

"Cover me!" said Tom to Elenna.

She drew Taladon's sword, and swung it left and right in long arcs. The Hounds drew back for a moment, then pressed in again.

"Whatever you need to do, do it quickly!" shouted Elenna.

Tom placed his hand over the

feather from the Flame Bird. *Epos!* he
willed. *I need you, old friend.* Elenna
thrust and slashed, driving back two
Hounds. Another dived at her, but
she ducked and the creature
sprawled into two of its pack. As the
others drew nearer, Tom searched the
crack of sky, feeling his hopes die.

"Your friend has deserted you!"
hissed Ravira. "Your Quest is over!"

CHAPTER FOUR

THIRST FOR BLOOD

From somewhere above, a screech cut the air. The chamber was cast in darkness, lit only by the orange glow from the lava beneath the white city and the fire licking over Epos's wings. Tom's heart lifted as he saw the glorious burnished feathers of the mighty Phoenix, and the golden beak sparkling in the moonlight.

"Epos!" Tom called.

"No!" roared Ravira. "Kill the Flame Bird!"

But the Hounds whined in fear and backed away, their red eyes glowing.

As Tom's eyes adjusted to the gloom, he saw Ravira searching the chamber ceiling with her gaze. "You won't defeat me!" she snarled, rattling the leashes. "Not like this!"

One Hound didn't seem as afraid as the others, and paced forwards. Taladon! His flanks heaved with muscle and his claws scraped the stone as he approached.

"I won't fight you," said Tom, unsure if his father could hear him.

The Hound growled, long strings of drool pooling beneath him. His hind legs bent slightly and Tom was ready as the creature leapt forward. He raised his shield and the Hound's jaws

clamped down on either side. It shook
its head from side to side, yanking the
shield from his arm. Tom fell back on
the ground as the Beast loomed over
him. His sword hilt rested in his hand.

"Father!" he said. "No…"

The Hound lunged, and Tom raised
the sword. He flinched as the blade
sliced into his father's side. The
monster fell like a sack of grain to
the ground beside him. As the blade
slipped out, blood gurgled from
a wound in the Hound's flank.

"What have I done?" Tom

mumbled. The Hound's eyes watched him in fear. "I had no choice."

"Tom!" Elenna called.

She was facing a wall of Hounds. They darted in and out, snapping with their jaws in a chorus of snarls.

"Don't stab!" said Tom, seizing up his shield and joining her side. "Just slash at them! They're innocent people, remember."

He looked again at the Hound that was his father, and saw him trying to stand in a pool of blood. *How long has he got before…?*

"Call off your Beasts," cursed Ravira, "and I'll spare your lives!"

Even out of the moonlight, she seemed powerful. But how?

"Never!" shouted Tom over the writhing wall of Hounds. He smashed his shield across a muzzle and the

monster howled in pain. Tom saw
a gap and darted through. He reached
the first step towards Ravira's throne
when his legs were yanked away
beneath him. He crashed into the
stone floor, and twisted to see a
Hound with its teeth gripping his
trouser leg. It dragged him on his
back across the ground, but he kicked
desperately with his other foot. His
heel caught its throat and the Hound
released him.

A shadow and the stench of rotten

fur rose up. Tom rolled as another of Ravira's creatures pounced. He swung the flat of his sword at its legs, sweeping them away, then sprang to his feet. Elenna backed towards him, spinning Taladon's sword in dizzying figures-of-eight to keep the growling Hounds at bay.

"It's no use," she panted. "There are too many of them."

Ravira hissed and cackled, wielding her leashes like whips and lashing the Hounds on. "That's right, my beauties! They're tiring – the kill is near!"

The leashes! Tom thought. *I have to try again.*

With his back to Elenna's, facing in opposite directions, he whispered to his friend. "I think her power is linked to the Hounds as well as the moonlight. The more Hounds she has, the stronger she is."

"We need to get closer," said Tom. "If I can help you past the Hounds, can you cut through the leashes?"

"I'll try," she said.

Tom roared a battle cry, and plunged at the pack, swinging wildly to drive them back. He let his sword drop to the stone floor and scraped the tip in a wide arc, sending up a shower of sparks. The Hounds retreated a few paces, whining in fear and frustration.

"Now!" Tom shouted.

Elenna took a few steps, then jumped high over one of the Hounds.

"Stop her!" screeched Ravira.

Elenna bounded up the steps towards Ravira, then leapt aside, bringing down her blade with both hands across the place where the chains were bundled together. The leashes burst apart.

"No!" Ravira hissed. She stepped down from her throne, and swung an arm, catching Elenna across the side of the face and sending her tumbling back down the steps with a cry of pain. The Beast's right arm still controlled several Hounds as she turned her yellow eyes on Tom.

"You'll pay for that!" Tom shouted.

He lifted his sword, and threw it in spinning arcs. The blade sliced through the remaining leashes and lodged in the wall of the chamber.

Ravira staggered and her hand caught the arm of her throne. Elenna stood, shaking her head groggily. Tom raised his shield to face the wall of Hounds but they no longer snarled. Their eyes, which had shone like beacons in the gloom, had faded to grey. They lowered their heads and their tails trailed between their legs.

"They're no longer under her control," Elenna shouted.

The pack slunk away to the edges of the chamber, and Tom rushed to his father's side.

"Taladon!" he cried.

The Hound's flanks were rising and falling but his eyes were half-closed and his tongue lolled weakly.

"Tom! Look out!" yelled Elenna.

He raised his shield, just as something flashed through the air towards his face. It struck the enchanted wood like a crack of thunder. When he lifted the shield away, he saw Ravira moving down the steps, her shroud rustling over the steps. She flicked her left hand, and the chains lashed at Elenna. His friend dove aside as the severed leashes fell onto the ground.

"You think you can defeat me?" roared Ravira. "I may be weakened but I'm still a match for you!" She swung the ragged leashes over her head and Tom ducked as they scythed the air.

Elenna rushed to his side and took his arm to pull him away. "We can't

stay here," she said.

Tom stood firm. "I won't leave my father," he said, as Ravira drifted across the chamber towards them. Her pale face twisted with anger and she raised her chin in defiance.

"She'll kill you," said Elenna. "We'll find another way to face her."

Elenna's right. Tom let her tug him back as the leashes sliced the air.

"I'll come back for you," he called to the dying Hound. Then they backed out of the chamber, leaving his father behind.

CHAPTER FIVE

A FIERY GRAVE

Ravira flicked her hands. The leashes crunched into the wall at Tom's side, showering him with dust and stone debris. "I'll crush your bones into powder!" called the Beast. Her fury seemed to shake the walls of the underworld. *How can we even get close?* Tom wondered.

Elenna leapt back as the chains

thumped down in front of her.

"We need to work together," Tom said. "If one of us can keep her busy, the other…"

He broke off as Ravira snapped her wrist and the chains swirled towards him. Tom lifted his shield and staggered under the blow. More trailing leashes swung at him. He ducked, lifting his sword. The chains looped around the blade.

Got you! Tom thought, twirling the sword to wrap the leashes further. He yanked hard, pulling Ravira off balance. Elenna darted closer, stabbing with Taladon's sword, but Ravira was ready. With a flick of her free hand, she swatted Elenna aside. When she stood again, Tom saw blood pouring from a cut in his friend's side where the leashes had shredded her tunic.

Ravira lashed with her trapped hand. Tom felt a jolt up his arm, bringing searing pain to his shoulder. But he held on and yanked, pulling Ravira into one of the city streets. She tried to lash again, but between the low buildings, there wasn't room to swing them. The Beast tried to whip at Elenna too, but Tom's friend caught the other leashes around her sword, just as he had done.

"Let me go!" Ravira cried. "Where are my Hounds? Come, my creatures! Sink your teeth into their flesh."

Tom saw the pack of Hounds, cowering near the gateway to the fortress. They sniffed the ground unsurely and didn't budge.

"They no longer heed you!" shouted Elenna.

Writing and bellowing in anguish, Ravira's pale green face twisted in the flickering red light from the lava river. She tried to pull them towards her, but Tom and Elenna stepped further back. With a screech of anger, Ravira tugged hard, and one set of chains fell loose from Tom's sword. Ravira took the other leashes in both hands and heaved Elenna off her feet.

Tom ran forwards as the Beast raised her thin arm, ready to cut his friend to ribbons with her whips. As the chains descended in a blur, he crouched beside Elenna and lifted his shield over both of them. The tip of the chains lashed over the top, a hair's breadth from his face.

Taking Elenna's hand, he helped her to her feet, and pulled her into

a side alley. The chains wrapped
around the edge, crumbling the wall.

"Run away, you pathetic creatures!"
bellowed Ravira.

Tom led Elenna back up the hill
a little, and then doubled back. "We
need to get behind her," he said.

"I'll find you," echoed Ravira's
voice. "You cannot escape me!"

Tom peered around a corner, and
saw the Beast stalking slowly down
the street, her chains dragging like an

army of snakes. Beyond her, the lava lake glowed. Tom put his finger to his lips and crept out after her. Both he and Elenna raised their swords. Thirty paces below, Tom saw the spot where the street widened beside the dock. The river seethed with molten rock. *If we can just get her closer…*

Ravira turned, and her eyes glowed the same colour as the river.

"You think you can sneak up on me?" she grinned.

"Tangle the chains again," said Tom.

"But she almost killed us last time," Elenna replied.

"Trust me!"

As Ravira lashed, they both raised their swords, and caught the ragged chains. "Come closer!" the Beast laughed, sensing victory. "Your swords are useless now!"

"Elenna," hissed Tom. "When I give the signal, run past her towards the river."

"What?" gasped Elenna.

"She'll give chase," Tom explained, "but won't want to end up in that lava. She'll be trapped. We'll have the better of her and she'll have no choice but to give in."

Elenna smiled grimly.

Ravira flexed her jagged nails. "I'll tear you to pieces with my claws." She twirled her hands, and wrapped the chains around her wrists, pulling them a pace closer.

"Now!" said Tom.

He ran straight at Ravira, and Elenna did the same. The Beast's eyes widened with sudden shock. When they were just a few paces away, Tom changed direction, running wide of

Ravira towards the river. The chains
pulled taut on both sides, dragging
Ravira with them. At the river's edge,
Tom skidded to a halt.

"There's nowhere to run!" he called
to the Beast. "Stop this fight."

With a panicked cry the Beast was
yanked towards the bank. Her arms
wheeled in the air as she struggled to
keep her balance. Her mouth gaped
with a scream of terror. But her
momentum was too much. Her

shroud caught fire and slowly she tipped into the current of lava, throwing up a curtain of molten rock. Her chains hissed and melted. Tom watched as the Beast thrashed to keep her face above the lava. Her struggles didn't last long and soon she sank beneath the surface.

"She's finished," gasped Elenna.

Tom felt pity, but then he tore his eyes from the molten flow, back up to the fortress. "Taladon!"

CHAPTER SIX

ESCAPE FROM THE UNDERWORLD

The cavern shook beneath Tom's feet, and he clutched Elenna. Cracking sounds split the air and showers of stone cascaded down. Some splashed into the river of lava, other pieces the size of his fist bounced off the white roads and roofs. "It's an earthquake!" Tom cried. "We'll be buried alive!"

They ran up through the streets

towards the fortress, with the whole Underworld kingdom shaking.

"How can we even get out?" asked Elenna. "Without the boatman, we can't cross the river."

"My father must have come a different way," said Tom.

At the fortress gates, the wall of Hounds blocked their path. The Hound in the middle suddenly stepped forwards towards him. Tom fought the urge to draw his sword.

"You're not evil, are you?" he whispered.

The giant creature lifted his muzzle, and Tom inched his hand closer. The Hound reached up, and sniffed. With a high-pitched whine, it dropped to its side. The others copied, sprawling across the stone, or rolling onto their backs.

Slowly, before Tom's eyes, the giant
dogs seemed to grow smaller, their
limbs changing shape with a sound
like breaking twigs. The muzzles
shrank back, the eyes moved closer
together and the faces gradually
resembled humans once more. Some
lay on their backs, others crouched
on all fours. The last thing to change
was their skin. Soon, a dozen people
in ragged and torn clothes were
staring at each other in confusion on
the ground.

"What happened?" asked one man.

"Where are we?" said another.

A pained groan sounded from inside the chamber.

Tom darted through the arched gateway. One of the fortress walls crumbled to pieces, and drove a cloud of dust over the floor.

"Father!"

Taladon lay on his side. The pool of blood from the injury in his side was sticky, but the wound had stopped bleeding. His skin was pale as fresh snow. Tom gripped his hand, only to find it cold. He took off his shield, and snatched the talon.

With a groan, a crack split open the ground, snaking up the steps to Ravira's throne.

"There isn't time," gasped Taladon. "You have to get out of here."

"I'm not leaving you," said Tom, holding the talon close to the wound.

The roof above creaked, and Tom looked up to see a rockfall heading towards him. He leant over his father's body as the pieces thumped across his back. Taladon suddenly gripped his arm, pushing the talon away. "Go, or you'll all be killed."

"Tom!" Elenna shouted. "Bo's here. He says he knows the way out."

Tom turned and saw a crowd of villagers with his friend. The tall boatman, Jacob's father, stood beside her. "There's a passage," he said.

With a crash, Ravira's throne toppled from its perch and smashed into pieces on the ground. Cracks snaked across the wall behind and it began to lean.

"Help me with my father!" Tom

shouted to Elenna.

His friend rushed to his side, and taking an arm each over their shoulders, they heaved Taladon to his feet. He moaned in pain. "We'll get you out soon," Tom said.

Staggering under the weight, they followed Bo and the people of Shrayton from the chamber. All across the underground city, buildings were collapsing and the roof showered boulders and rubble. The crash and crunch of rock on rock was deafening.

Bo led them along a low passage, taking turns left and right.

"Are you sure you know where you're going?" shouted a villager.

Tom shared an anxious look with Elenna. Sweat glistened as they half-carried, half-dragged Taladon at the

back of the group.

"This way!" cried Bo, pointing up a spiral stone staircase. He went first and the villagers followed in a panicked chain. There wasn't room for three people side by side.

"You go ahead!" said Tom to his friend.

Elenna did as he asked, and Tom lifted his father over his shoulder.

The whole staircase shook violently from side to side, and the sound of the destruction below reverberated in his ears. With each step up, the burden seemed heavier, but Tom concentrated on putting one foot in front of the other.

"Almost there!" called Elenna. Tom saw light above. Bo was reaching back through a trapdoor, pulling up the last of the villagers. A crashing made Tom look back. Five steps down, the steps collapsed into emptiness. Below he saw the ruins of the white city. He was almost level with the cavern roof, when he heard Ravira's final words again, like the whisper of a distant wind.

This place will be your grave!

Tom slipped as the step he was standing on gave way. He staggered

up the few remaining steps towards
the Avantian sky. Elenna's legs
disappeared through the hole.

"Take Taladon," Tom gasped,
pushing his father's body up with all
his strength. Strong hands gripped
Taladon's clothes and arms, and
pulled him up.

"Give me your hand!" said Elenna.

Tom had nothing left. He tried to lift
his arm, but at the same moment, he
felt the ground slip away. *I'm falling!*

CHAPTER SEVEN

A PEACEFUL KINGDOM

Something closed on his tunic, and Tom found himself scooped from the air and lifted as though he weighed nothing, out into the cool air. He heard a screech, and saw the dark silhouette of Epos's fiery wings, beating with powerful strokes. The Flame Bird's talons clutched him.

The Good Beast laid him carefully

on the dusty ground.

"Thank you!" said Tom, climbing to his feet, and laying a hand on Epos's feathers. A few paces away a cluster of people crowded round a body. "There's nothing we can do for him," said Bo.

Tom pushed past to the centre, where Taladon lay wounded. He took the talon from his shield again and crouched at his father's side, pulling aside his bloody tunic. He held the talon over the wound. At first nothing happened, and Taladon arched his back in pain. Tom held his breath. *Please! This has to work...*

"What's he doing?" Bo asked.

Slowly, the edges of the cut drew together, sealing the puncture. Tom breathed again with relief, as the skin became smooth.

"It's a miracle!" said another villager.

Taladon sat up weakly. "You did it, Tom," he croaked. "I'm proud of you."

Tom looked about him at the pale grey sky, where the moon was a disc streaked with cloud. They were standing in a wide glen. The sun would be up soon.

"We had a little help," he said, smiling.

The rescued villagers stared as

Ferno and Epos flew in low swoops around them.

The sound of hooves made Tom turn. Riding towards them on Storm was Jacob. Fleetfoot cantered beside them and Silver bounded through the dawn excitedly.

"Your horse wouldn't stop whinnying!" said Jacob. "He seemed to know you'd be here!"

"My son!" said Bo.

Jacob slipped from the saddle and threw his arms around his father.

Tom stood, patting his faithful stallion's neck. "Where are we?"

Bo pointed to a trail of smoke in the air over the swell of a hill. "We're just east of Shrayton," he said. "At the old mines. Let's get back to the village."

Tom walked to the trapdoor. He

could see nothing in the abyss below. No white stone, no river of lava. Not a sound came from the darkness. He closed the trapdoor gratefully.

He trudged across the grass with his father and Elenna, while the villagers rushed ahead. As they entered the outskirts of Shrayton, village-folk, young and old, emerged from the boarded-up houses, and ran towards the new arrivals. Many still carried their makeshift weapons, but they dropped them or threw them aside when they saw the threat from the Hounds had gone. There were excited shouts and tears of joy as the villagers embraced one another.

By the village well, Tom stopped with his father.

"I can't stop thinking what might have happened if Ravira had escaped," he said.

"Avantia's Underworld is the darkest place," said a voice. The three of them turned as one to see Aduro standing walking behind them. "But I trust that, with heroes such as you fighting for it, the kingdom would have been well protected if it happened."

"It still might," added Taladon. "The Underworld holds unknowable secrets that we may one day discover. But today is not that day – thanks to you."

Tom felt his face flush with pride at his father's praise. "You know…I never meant to stab you – when you were a Hound. It's just that…"

His father put his hand on Tom's shoulder. "You did what you had to do," he said. "As any true warrior should."

Tom nodded, and Elenna undid her
sword belt. "I think you should have
this back," she said, smiling. "I prefer
my bow and arrows."

Tom noticed that her teeth had
returned to normal, and checked his
hands. Sure enough, the hairs had
vanished and his nails had shrunk to
normal size. Checking his arm, he
saw that the tooth marks from the
Hound had melted away.

"The curse has gone," he muttered.

The first rays of dawn spilled across the sky, picking out the banks of low-lying cloud. "I'm looking forward to going back home," Tom said. "Aunt Maria and Uncle Henry won't believe what's happened."

A gurgling sound startled him. "It's coming from the well," said Elenna.

Together, they peered in. The early morning light caught the glimmer of water below. It was as clear as a mirror and bubbled freshly as the line of water rose up the stone walls. "The well is filling up!" said Tom.

"Life will return to Shrayton now Ravira has gone," Aduro said.

A roar above them made Tom's skin tingle. Ferno glided overheard, his black-scaled tail and mighty wings propelling him. Ferno followed in a sweep of flaming feathers.

"Farewell, friends!" called Tom. The villagers stared upwards in astonishment as the two Good Beasts soared over the village until they became distant dots, side by side.

Tom placed his foot in Storm's stirrups and pulled himself up into the saddle. Elenna climbed up behind him, and Storm wagged his tail with excitement.

"I can use my magic to send you home, if you wish," said Aduro. "It's a day's ride, at least."

"I'd rather ride," said Tom.

"So would I," Elenna added.

Tom smiled at Aduro. "We want to see Avantia again. After all, we nearly lost it."

JOIN TOM ON HIS NEXT
BEAST QUEST SOON!

Win an exclusive
Beast Quest T-shirt and goody bag!

Tom has battled many fearsome Beasts and we want to know
which one is your favourite! Send us a drawing or painting of
your favourite Beast and tell us in 30 words why you think
it's the best.

Each month we will select **three** winners to receive
a Beast Quest T-shirt and goody bag!

Send your entry on a postcard to
BEAST QUEST COMPETITION
Orchard Books, 338 Euston Road, London NW1 3BH.

Australian readers should email:
childrens.books@hachette.com.au

New Zealand readers should write to:
Beast Quest Competition, PO Box 3255, Shortland St,
Auckland 1140, NZ or email: childrensbooks@hachette.co.nz

**Don't forget to include your name and address.
Only one entry per child.**

Good luck!

Join the Quest,
Join the Tribe

www.beastquest.co.uk

Have you checked out the Beast Quest website?
It's the place to go for games, downloads, activities,
sneak previews and lots of fun!

You can read all about your favourite Beasts, down-
load free screensavers and desktop wallpapers for
your computer, and even challenge your friends
to a Beast Tournament.

Sign up to the newsletter at www.beastquest.co.uk
to receive exclusive extra content and the oppor-
tunity to enter special members-only competitions.
We'll send you up-to-date info on all the Beast
Quest books, including the next exciting series
which features six brand-new Beasts!

Get 30% off all Beast Quest Books at www.beastquest.co.uk
Enter the code BEAST at the checkout.

- [ ] 1. Ferno the Fire Dragon
- [ ] 2. Sepron the Sea Serpent
- [ ] 3. Arcta the Mountain Giant
- [ ] 4. Tagus the Horse-Man
- [ ] 5. Nanook the Snow Monster
- [ ] 6. Epos the Flame Bird

Beast Quest:
The Golden Armour
- [ ] 7. Zepha the Monster Squid
- [ ] 8. Claw the Giant Monkey
- [ ] 9. Soltra the Stone Charmer
- [ ] 10. Vipero the Snake Man
- [ ] 11. Arachnid the King of Spiders
- [ ] 12. Trillion the Three-Headed Lion

Beast Quest:
The Dark Realm
- [ ] 13. Torgor the Minotaur
- [ ] 14. Skor the Winged Stallion
- [ ] 15. Narga the Sea Monster
- [ ] 16. Kaymon the Gorgon Hound
- [ ] 17. Tusk the Mighty Mammoth
- [ ] 18. Sting the Scorpion Man

Beast Quest:
The Amulet of Avantia
- [ ] 19. Nixa the Death Bringer
- [ ] 20. Equinus the Spirit Horse
- [ ] 21. Rashouk the Cave Troll
- [ ] 22. Luna the Moon Wolf
- [ ] 23. Blaze the Ice Dragon
- [ ] 24. Stealth the Ghost Panther

Beast Quest:
The Shade of Death
- [ ] 25. Krabb Master of the Sea
- [ ] 26. Hawkite Arrow of the Air
- [ ] 27. Rokk the Walking Mountain
- [ ] 28. Koldo the Arctic Warrior
- [ ] 29. Trema the Earth Lord
- [ ] 30. Amictus the Bug Queen

Beast Quest:
The World of Chaos
- [ ] 31. Komodo the Lizard King
- [ ] 32. Muro the Rat Monster
- [ ] 33. Fang the Bat Fiend
- [ ] 34. Murk the Swamp Man
- [ ] 35. Terra Curse of the Forest
- [ ] 36. Vespick the Wasp Queen

Beast Quest:
The Lost World
- [ ] 37. Convol the Cold-Blooded Brute
- [ ] 38. Hellion the Fiery Foe
- [ ] 39. Krestor the Crushing Terror
- [ ] 40. Madara the Midnight Warrior
- [ ] 41. Ellik the Lightning Horror
- [ ] 42. Carnivora the Winged Scavenger

Beast Quest:
The Pirate King
- [ ] 43. Balisk the Water Snake
- [ ] 44. Koron Jaws of Death
- [ ] 45. Hecton the Body Snatcher
- [ ] 46. Torno the Hurricane Dragon
- [ ] 47. Kronus the Clawed Menace
- [ ] 48. Bloodboar the Buried Doom

Beast Quest:
The Warlock's Staff
- [ ] 49. Ursus the Clawed Roar
- [ ] 50. Minos the Demon Bull
- [ ] 51. Koraka the Winged Assassin
- [ ] 52. Silver the Wild Terror
- [ ] 53. Spikefin the Water King
- [ ] 54. Torpix the Twisting Serpent

Beast Quest:
Master of the Beasts
- [ ] 55. Noctila the Death Owl
- [ ] 56. Shamani the Raging Flame
- [ ] 57. Lustor the Acid Dart
- [ ] 58. Voltrex the Two-Headed Octopus
- [ ] 59. Tecton the Armoured Giant
- [ ] 60. Doomskull the King of Fear

Beast Quest:
The New Age
- [ ] 61. Elko Lord of the Sea
- [ ] 62. Tarrok the Blood Spike
- [ ] 63. Brutus the Hound of Horror
- [ ] 64. Flaymar the Scorched Blaze
- [ ] 65. Serpio the Slithering Shadow
- [ ] 66. Tauron the Pounding Fury

Beast Quest:
The Darkest Hour
- [ ] 67. Solak Scourge of the Sea
- [ ] 68. Kajin the Beast Catcher
- [ ] 69. Issrilla the Creeping Menace
- [ ] 70. Vigrash the Clawed Eagle
- [ ] 71. Mirka the Ice Horse
- [ ] 72. Kama the Faceless Beast

Special Bumper Editions
- [ ] Vedra & Krimon: Twin Beasts of Avantia
- [ ] Spiros the Ghost Phoenix
- [ ] Arax the Soul Stealer
- [ ] Kragos & Kildor: The Two-Headed Demon
- [ ] Creta the Winged Terror
- [ ] Mortaxe the Skeleton Warrior
- [ ] Ravira, Ruler of the Underworld
- [ ] Raksha the Mirror Demon
- [ ] Grashkor the Beast Guard
- [ ] Ferrok the Iron Soldier

All books priced at £4.99.
Special bumper editions priced at £5.99.

Orchard Books are available from all good bookshops, or can
be ordered from our website: www.orchardbooks.co.uk,
or telephone 01235 827702, or fax 01235 8227703.

Series 8: THE PIRATE KING OUT NOW!

Sanpao the Pirate King plans to steal the sacred Tree of Being. Can Tom scupper his wicked intentions?

978 1 40831 310 7

978 1 40831 311 4

978 1 40831 312 1

978 1 40831 313 8

978 1 40831 314 5

978 1 40831 315 2

Series 9: The Warlock's Staff
Out September 2011

Ursus the Clawed Roar
Minos the Demon Bull
Koraka the Winged Assassin
Silver the Wild Terror
Spikefin the Water King
Torpix the Twisting Serpent

**Watch out for the next
Special Bumper
Edition**

OUT OCTOBER 2011!

RAVIRA
THE RULER OF THE UNDERWORLD

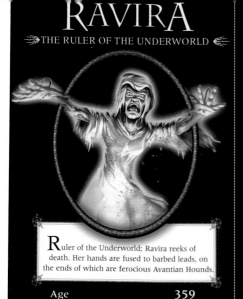

Ruler of the Underworld; Ravira reeks of death. Her hands are fused to barbed leads, on the ends of which are ferocious Avantian Hounds.

Age	359
Power	291
Magic Level	190
Fright Factor	91

FLEETFOOT

Taladon's trusty stallion Fleetfoot is brave and fast, and understands exactly what Taladon needs him to do.

Age	30
Power	250
Magic Level	89
Fright Factor	50

HOUNDS
OF AVANTIA

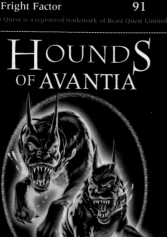

Just one bite from Ravira's terrifying servants will turn their victim into a slave.

Age	2
Power	226
Magic Level	171
Fright Factor	98

THE
UNDERWORLD

A dark and terrifying place; Ravira's lair under the surface of Avantia.

Age	473
Power	203
Magic Level	116
Fright Factor	68

Fight the Beasts,
Fear the Magic

www.beastquest.co.uk
ORCHARD BOOKS

Fight the Beasts,
Fear the Magic

www.beastquest.co.uk
ORCHARD BOOKS

Fight the Beasts,
Fear the Magic

www.beastquest.co.uk
ORCHARD BOOKS

Fight the Beasts,
Fear the Magic

www.beastquest.co.uk
ORCHARD BOOKS